MW01077282

Praise for *Adeline by the Sea*

"*Adeline by the Sea* is a tender portrait of the small moments that shape us into braver beings. The gentle narrator, Henry ("Bones"), transported me to the familiar bliss of childhood beach vacations, when my experiences each day inched me toward a greater understanding of how grown-ups and the wider world work, and how nature and family ground us all. Author Lauren Oakey and illustrator Britt Van Deusen share a gift for capturing the poignancy and wonder of these early moments in our lives. They have created a book that kids and adults can enjoy over and over again."

—Meaghan Rady, executive producer of *Brené Brown: Atlas of the Heart*

"*Adeline by the Sea* is a celebration of morning glories, purple martins, and precious beach time with family—but it's much more than that. In *Adeline by the Sea*, a story as expansive and solid as a wraparound porch, Henry learns what it means to be a proud grandson, a protective brother to his little sister, and a person who will cheer on loved ones when they want to take wing and fly."

—Mary E. Cronin, poet, writer, and literacy coach

"Vivid imagery and beautiful illustrations tell a heartwarming story of family, love, and hope. It's impossible not to root for Henry as he learns what it means to be brave, and readers of all ages will appreciate the emotional and optimistic ending."

—Stacy Hackney, author of *Forever Glimmer Creek* and *The Sisters of Luna Island*

"*Adeline by the Sea* is a beautiful portrait of a family creating lasting memories at the beach and is full of details that allow the reader to feel just how special each moment together is. It is also a story of a loving brother learning to cope with his feelings of protectiveness and worry, and the special relationships that help him to do so. Through the delightful illustrations and peaceful prose, the story allows children to connect with the common emotions and experiences shared by families, and to remember that letting go is an important part of growing up."

—Kelsey Felton, school counselor

Adeline by the Sea

BELLE ISLE BOOKS
www.belleislebooks.com

Story by
Lauren Oakey

Illustrations by
Britt Van Deusen

Copyright © 2023 by Lauren Oakey

No part of this book may be reproduced in any form or by any electronic or mechanical means, or the facilitation thereof, including information storage and retrieval systems, without permission in writing from the publisher, except in the case of brief quotations published in articles and reviews. Any educational institution wishing to photocopy part or all of the work for classroom use, or individual researchers who would like to obtain permission to reprint the work for educational purposes, should contact the publisher

ISBN: 978-1-958754-49-8
Library of Congress Control Number: 2023904139

Designed by Sami Langston
Production managed by Haley Simpkiss

Printed in the United States of America

Published by
Belle Isle Books (an imprint of Brandylane Publishers, Inc.)
5 S. 1st Street
Richmond, Virginia 23219

BELLE ISLE BOOKS
www.belleislebooks.com

belleislebooks.com | brandylanepublishers.com

For Stedman and the von Oesen family

– LO

For Marla and Winnie

– BVD

Every summer . . .

when Mama feels the pull of the ocean . . .

Daddy takes us all to the coast.

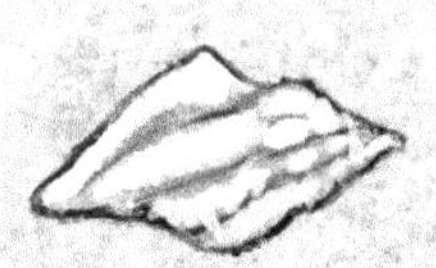

That's where Nana and Grandpa – Daddy's grandparents – live, on the coast of North Carolina. Nana passed away years ago, but the house is still "Nana and Grandpa's," and visits to the beach mean we hear stories about her. Mama says that she always kept fresh blueberries and milk in the refrigerator when they would visit and that she loved to spend time in her garden. The pink and white morning glories that Grandpa planted for her still grow by the kitchen window.

The house is just off the main strip at the beach, on the same small street as the Presbyterian church. It faces the street but sits right on the sound. What a funny name for water, *the sound.*

But the sound gives us the view that Daddy loves most, best seen from the giant wraparound porch that stretches around three sides of the house.

We look across the water to a row of colorful houses and to the two short bridges – one far to the left and one far to the right – that bring you over to the beach. There are also plenty of chairs for rocking, and a birdhouse just for purple martins at the back-right corner of the yard. It's so close to the porch, you can almost touch it.

Grandpa knows a lot about purple martins, like they eat and drink while flying, and they aren't actually purple – they're iridescent – which means their feathers just shimmer in a way that makes them look purple. They come every summer to have their babies right here next to the house, and I spend a few minutes each morning watching the chicks being fed. I like to make sure that they're being taken care of – I don't like the thought of them being hungry for long.

Adeline, my little sister, she likes to watch them too. Mama will send us up to the porch with our breakfast, and we each find a rocker to sit in. Then we watch and eat. Alice, my big sister, she'll come up too, but she always has her nose in a book and lies down in the hammock. That's just fine by me, because that means she stays put. Adeline always gets up and stands on the railings, trying to reach the bird house. I have to get up and pull her back so she doesn't go flying off the porch.

I'm named after Grandpa – we're both Henry – but no one calls me that. Everyone calls me Bones. I don't mind either way, but Grandpa says Henry is "a good, strong name," and I believe him, because I don't know anyone tougher than Grandpa. He is over six feet tall; he was a colonel in the army, and when he talks, we all stop to listen. Secretly, I love that we share a name; that we share anything makes me feel braver.

Each day at the beach, we fall into the same routine. In the morning we walk across the main road to the beach, and when we reach the sand, we throw off our flip-flops and head straight for the ocean. Alice and I love to play a game called "over-under." When a wave comes rolling toward us, we decide which way we're gonna take it – jump over it, or dive under.

Adeline wants to play too, but she's too little. Daddy lets her sit in the surf and play, or wade in the water up to her knees, but I always ask him to watch her more closely. What if a big wave grabs her? Or what if she falls? Sometimes, if the waves are coming fast, I quit playing over-under and take Adeline to look for seashells.

That way I can be sure she's safe. She doesn't talk much – she never has – but when she points and says, "Look!" I know she's found a favorite. We like to collect those in her bucket and use them in our sandcastles for decoration. Alice likes to take them and make mermaid tails, too.

Mama says that it's better to go ahead and feel things than to put our feelings away, but I feel things deep, right down to my bones. And my little sister, well . . . I feel like she's mine to protect.

When the sun gets too hot, we walk back to the house to eat lunch and then rest. By this time, the streets have soaked up so much sun that they're especially hot, and I tell Adeline to walk on the white lines of the parking spaces along the street. They're not as hot. I carry her bucket for her too, just in case.

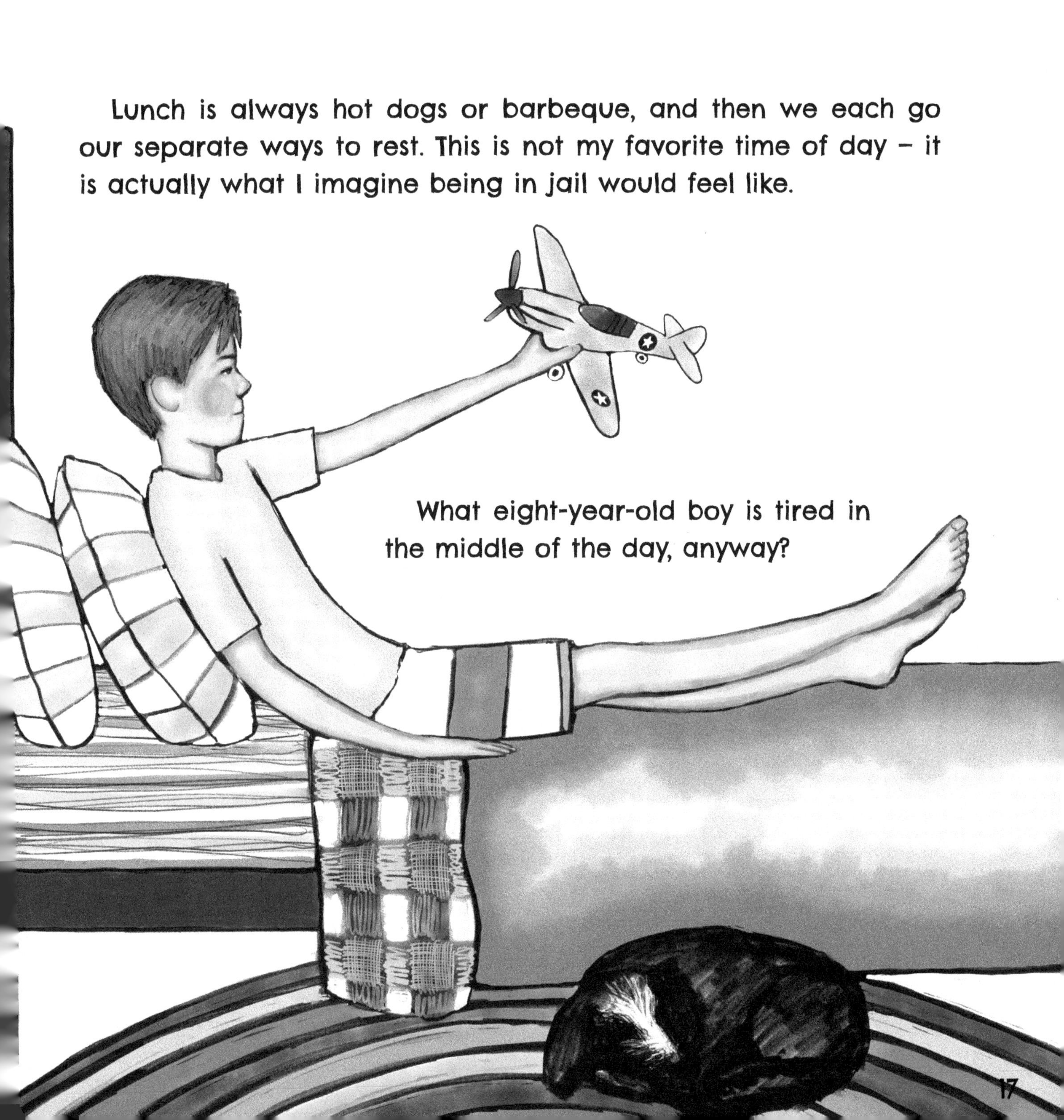
Lunch is always hot dogs or barbeque, and then we each go our separate ways to rest. This is not my favorite time of day – it is actually what I imagine being in jail would feel like.
What eight-year-old boy is tired in the middle of the day, anyway?

Today, I hear Mama and Grandpa out on the porch, and I think I hear Adeline, too. Why isn't she resting? How is that fair? So I decide on a jailbreak, praying Grandpa doesn't send me back to my room. I open the door slowly and peek out, and Grandpa says, "Oh, are you joining your little sister? Adeline gave up on rest time, too."

"Yes, sir." I say. And then I hear Adeline squealing off in the distance somewhere. Alarmed, I pop out onto the porch and look around, thinking she might be at the end near the purple martins. But she's out on the pier.

Alone.

"Adeline wants to jump out into the sound," Mama says. "To Daddy."

I do not think this is a good idea. She's only four and the water is deep. What if she slips out of Daddy's hands? And besides, the sound is covered in sharp oyster shells along the sand and barnacles along the pilings holding up the pier. What are they thinking?

I sit down reluctantly, keeping one eye on Adeline as she runs up and down the edge of the pier, Daddy right below her in the water. Mama and Grandpa continue talking about people I don't know and things I don't understand, but I'm not really listening anyway.

And then Grandpa looks at me and says, "Come here, Bones. I've got a secret for you."

I thought we weren't supposed to tell secrets in a group, so I look over at Mama, but she nods and says, "Go on, it's okay. Grandpa tells the best secrets."

I hop up and walk over to him with my back to Mama. He pulls me gently toward him and says in a real low voice, "You know, worrying about people feels a lot like loving 'em, but it's not the same thing. You gotta let 'em fly."

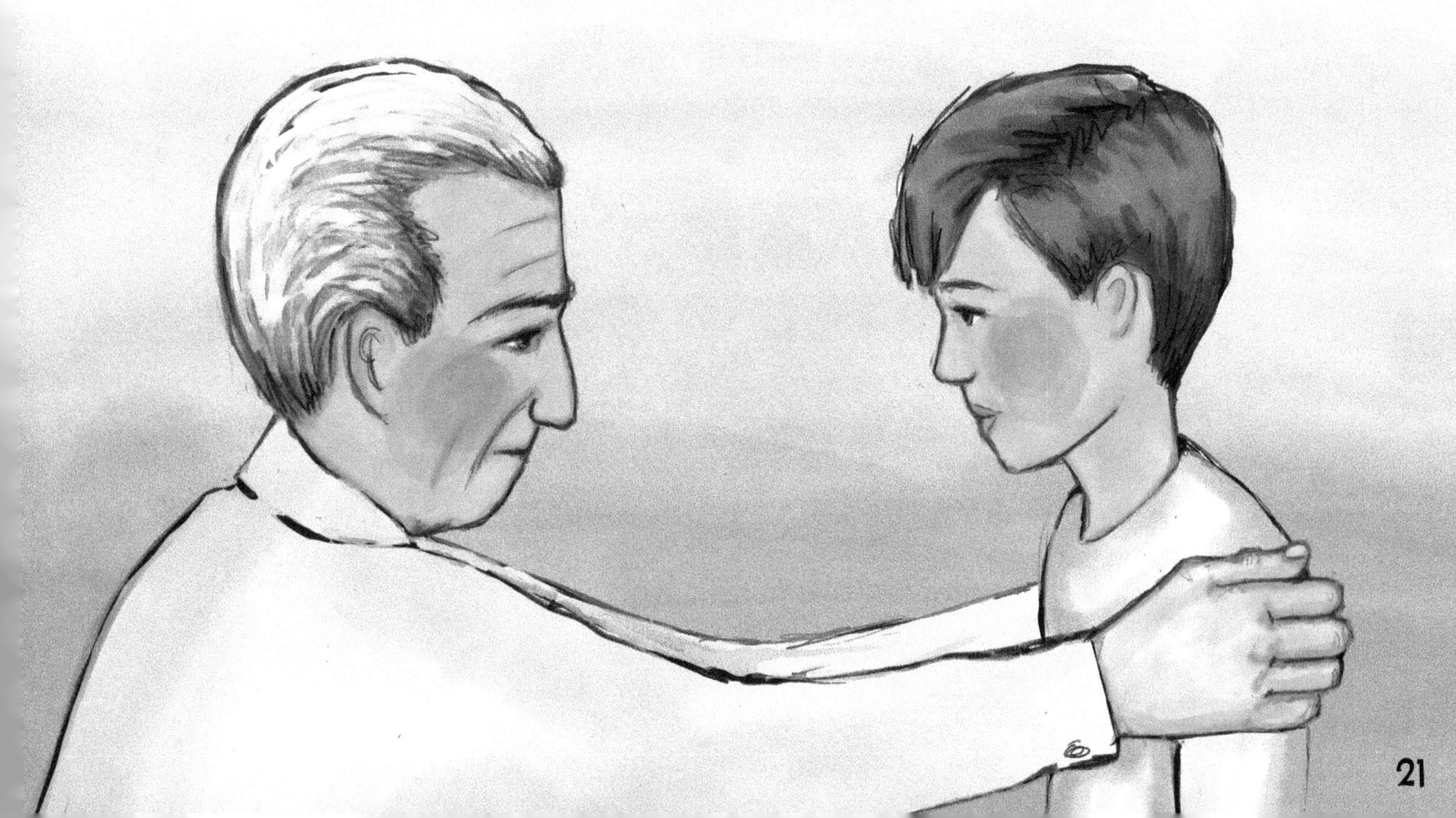

As he says this, I look past him at the martins. They're swooping and swirling and diving and gliding, scooping up water from the sound. And there's Adeline, right below them on the pier, getting ready to jump.

Something in me shifts. I run to the end of the porch and yell as loud as I can, "Jump, Adeline! Jump! You can do it!"

With that, she looks at me, then back at the water, and she takes off – her legs tucked under her just like a bird, her arms stretched out like wings, landing with a giant splash in the water. Daddy catches her. And then she climbs out and does it again and again and again and again. She's so proud of herself.

Later that evening, I find Grandpa up on the porch, staring out at the sunset – Nana's sunsets, he calls them; one of her favorite times of day.

I sit down next to him in a rocker and see the purple martins flying around the bird house, settling in for the evening.

"They'll be headed south soon," he says. "All the way to Brazil."

"That's so far," I say. "How do they know how to get there?" I can hear Adeline laughing inside the house and say, "Wait. What about the babies?"

"What about them?" Grandpa says.

"What if they aren't ready to fly that far?" I ask.

He keeps his eyes on the sunset and says, "Henry, it's all instinct. They trust that they'll know what to do. That everything will be ok."

He called me Henry. I feel braver. I sit up straighter.

I look right at him, smile, and say, "I bet they feel it right down in their bones."

About the Author

Lauren Tweel Oakey lives in Richmond, Virginia, and is a graduate of the University of Virginia, where she studied world religions and Italian language. She has lived in Italy and Switzerland, has worked mostly in non-profits, and is a lover of language and the rhythm of words. She also enjoys playing piano; practicing yoga; and spending time with her husband, three children, and very beautiful but high-maintenance black Lab.

About the Illustrator

Britt Van Deusen is an artist who lives in Richmond, Virginia, with her husband and three girls (two human and one canine). Britt studied painting at the College of William & Mary and the Marchutz School in France, and she has been a portrait artist for many years. When she is not making art, Britt often reads books that feature both people and animals in starring roles; regularly cooks somewhat fancy meals; occasionally plays silly songs on her guitar; and with stunning frequency, discovers birds' nests abandoned in nature.

CPSIA information can be obtained
at www.ICGtesting.com
Printed in the USA
LVHW071543300623
751251LV00011B/118